HOMEPLACE

A Richard Jackson Book

HOMEPLACE

by **Anne Shelby**

illustrations by **Wendy Anderson Halperin**

Orchard Books   New York

Orchard Books, 95 Madison Avenue, New York, NY 10016

Manufactured in the United States of America. Printed by Barton Press, Inc.
Bound by Horowitz/Rae. Book design by Mina Greenstein.
The text of this book is set in 16 point Cochin. The illustrations are pencil and watercolor
reproduced in full color. 10 9 8 7 6 5 4 3

Library of Congress Cataloging-in-Publication Data
Shelby, Anne. Homeplace / by Anne Shelby ; illustrated by Wendy Anderson Halperin.
p.   cm. "A Richard Jackson book" — Half t.p.
Summary: A grandmother and grandchild trace their family history.
ISBN 0-531-06882-X.   ISBN 0-531-08732-8 (lib. bdg.)
[1. Genealogy — Fiction.   2. Family life — Fiction.]   I. Halperin, Wendy Anderson, ill.
II. Title.   III. Title: Home place. PZ7.S54125Ho   1995   [E] — dc20   94-24856

To Lynne

— A.S.

For Kale, Joel, Lane, Lyric, and Zephyr

— W.A.H.

Your great-great-great-great-grandpa
built this house.

He cleared this land.
He used the best logs to build a sturdy cabin.
He saved the best stones for a fireplace
and chimney.

Then he planted corn.

Your great-great-great-great-grandma baked
corn bread on the fireplace stones.
She carried clothes to the river to scrub
them on flat rocks.

She put the babies to sleep on
a corn-shuck bed.
ONE of the babies . . .

W as your great-great-great-grandpa.
He grew like corn in the field,
like hollyhocks around the cabin.
Then he cleared more land.

He planted wheat fields and sweet sorghum for molasses.

He put up fences for sheep and cattle.

And built more rooms onto the cabin.

Your great-great-great-grandma spun sheep's wool on a wheel to make warm shirts and britches.

She strung dried beans and apples to save for winter suppers.

She stitched quilts to
wrap the babies in.
ONE of the babies . . .

Was your great-great-grandpa.
He grew like wheat stalks, like sunflowers
at the edge of the garden.

He plowed the fields with horses.

And built a porch to sit on, when the plowing got done.

Your great-great-grandma built fires
in the cookstove and under the wash kettle.
    She ordered a wicker rocker from a catalog,
then papered the walls with catalog pages.

At night she rocked the babies in the new
rocking chair and sang them
old songs to make them sleepy.
ONE of the babies . . .

W as your great-grandma.
She grew like a bean vine up a pole,
like honeysuckle on a fencerow.
      She helped your great-grandpa plow
with the tractor.

e helped her with the canning.
Together they lined the cellar shelves with
shiny jars of peaches and tomatoes.

They put the babies in the car
and took them for a ride.

ONE of the babies . . .

Was *me*.
I grew like a weed
after rain.
Then it was mine and
your grandpa's time to take
care of the old homeplace.
And time for it to take
care of us.

We added on a greenhouse and a playhouse for the babies. *ONE* of the babies . . .

Was your mother.
  She grew like a willow on the creek bank,
  like a wild rose in the woods.
  She and your daddy fixed the old chimney
  and built a fire in the fireplace again.

They peeled off wallpaper and catalog pages,
and there were the old logs—still good as new.
And, oh, I almost forgot. They built
on a nursery for the babies.
ONE of the babies was . . .

Y ou!

And now, here you are, growing like a melon in the patch, like tulips in the springtime of the year,

1810 1810 1850 1850 1850 1850 1880 1880

like a young tree coming up from old roots,
deep down in the ground.

880 1880 1880 1880 1910 1910 1950 1995

HOMEPLACE